READY for ANYTHING!

KEIKO KASZA

G.P.Putnam's Sons • Penguin Young Readers Group

To Mr. Uraki at Saera Shobou
who believed in me first.

G. P. PUTNAM'S SONS
A division of Penguin Young Readers Group. Published by The Penguin Group.
Penguin Group (USA) Inc., 375 Hudson Street, New York, NY 10014, U.S.A.
Penguin Group (Canada), 90 Eglinton Avenue East, Suite 700, Toronto, Ontario M4P 2Y3, Canada (a division of Pearson Penguin Canada Inc.).
Penguin Books Ltd, 80 Strand, London WC2R 0RL, England.
Penguin Ireland, 25 St. Stephen's Green, Dublin 2, Ireland (a division of Penguin Books Ltd.).
Penguin Group (Australia), 250 Camberwell Road, Camberwell, Victoria 3124, Australia (a division of Pearson Australia Group Pty Ltd).
Penguin Books India Pvt Ltd, 11 Community Centre, Panchsheel Park, New Delhi - 110 017, India.
Penguin Group (NZ), 67 Apollo Drive, Rosedale, North Shore 0632, New Zealand (a division of Pearson New Zealand Ltd).
Penguin Books (South Africa) (Pty) Ltd, 24 Sturdee Avenue, Rosebank, Johannesburg 2196, South Africa.
Penguin Books Ltd, Registered Offices: 80 Strand, London WC2R 0RL, England.

Design by Marikka Tamura. Text set in Greco. The art was done in gouache on three-ply bristol illustration paper.
Library of Congress Cataloging-in-Publication Data
Kasza, Keiko. Ready for anything! / Keiko Kasza.   p. cm.
Summary: Raccoon is nervous about all of the things that could spoil a picnic, from bees to dragons, until Duck convinces him that
surprises can be fun. [1. Worry—Fiction. 2. Picnicking—Fiction. 3. Raccoon—Fiction. 4. Ducks—Fiction.] I. Title.
PZ7.K15645Wgp 2009   [E1—dc22   2008033615
ISBN 978-0-399-25235-8
1 3 5 7 9 10 8 6 4 2

Duck arrived at Raccoon's house on a bright, sunny day.

"Hey, Raccoon!" said Duck. "Are you ready for our picnic?"

"Umm, well . . . I changed my mind," said Raccoon. "I don't want to go."

"Why not?" asked Duck.

"Well, I've been thinking," said Raccoon. "What if we are attacked by killer bees?"

"No . . . ," said Duck.

"Yeah," said Raccoon. "And what if they chase us, you know, and we fall into a river?"

"Oh, no," cried Duck.

"Oh, yeah," said Raccoon. "And what if we swim for our lives, but a terrible storm strikes?"

"Oh, no! Oh, no!" yelled Duck.

"Oh, yeah! Oh, yeah!" Raccoon went on. "And what if we look for shelter in a cave, but there's already someone in there, someone really scary?"

"Like . . . like who?" asked Duck.

"A DRAGON!!!!!"

shouted Raccoon.

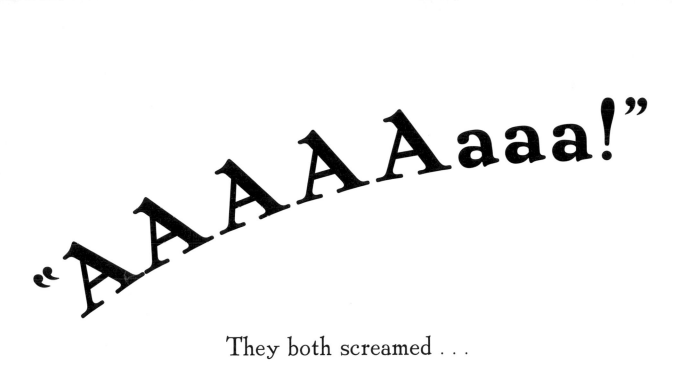

"AAAAAaaa!"

They both screamed . . .

. . . and they hid under a blanket.
"It could happen, you know," Raccoon warned.
"Picnics are dangerous."

"You're right." Duck thought about it for a while.
"But Raccoon . . .

. . . what if some lovely butterflies pass by instead of bees?"

"Hmm, that would be nice," said Raccoon.

"Yes," said Duck. "And what if we follow the butterflies to the river and jump in for a cool splash?"

"That would be even nicer,"
Raccoon answered.

"Yes, much nicer," Duck said. "And what if the weather is beautiful, with just a gentle breeze blowing? We could fly a kite!"

"Gee, that sounds like fun!" Raccoon admitted.

"Lots of fun!" Duck said. "And then,
we might find a cave to explore."

"Don't go in!" Raccoon shouted. "There's
a fire-breathing dragon in there! Remember?"

"Maybe," said Duck. "But what if it's just a cute little dragon who wants to play with us?"

"You think?" said Raccoon.

"Sure," said Duck. "And what if we have
the best picnic ever, roasting marshmallows?"

"Wow!" said Raccoon. "Your what-ifs
are wonderful, Duck."

"What are we waiting for?" Raccoon cried. "Let's go on a picnic!"

"That's the spirit, Raccoon!" Duck cheered.

"Just give me a few minutes to get ready," said Raccoon.

So Duck waited . . .

And waited . . .

And waited
some more . . .

Until finally
Raccoon announced,
"Okay, Duck,
I'm ready to go!"

"Oh, Raccoon." Duck fell over, laughing.
"You worry too much. But I guess you
are ready for anything, huh?"

At last the two friends left for their picnic.

"Thanks, Duck," said Raccoon. "This is much more fun than hiding under a blanket."

"No problem," said Duck. "Trust me. Nothing could go wrong on a little picnic."

But when they got there . . . Duck gasped!
"**OH, NO!**" Duck moaned. "**I FORGOT
THE PICNIC BASKET!**"
Duck wanted to cry, but Raccoon stayed calm.
"No problem," Raccoon declared, opening his backpack.
"Like you said . . .

... I'm ready for anything!"